DARIUS AND THE DOZER BULL

DARIUS

and the DOZER BULL

BY
Eleanor Harder

DRAWINGS BY DAVID K. STONE

Nashville   Abingdon Press   New York

TO RAY

1

Tharump! Whoompp! Grunk!

"What is *that?*" Darius dropped his pen and jumped to his rear feet.

Rr—Rr—Rr Whoompp! The long, sloping tunnel shook and the caves at the end where Darius lived echoed and rang to the noise.

"Swounds! Is it another earthquake? Every hundred years—it's too much."

Rr—Rr—Rr Whomp Whomp Bang! He felt the walls as they shook. It was no earthquake. Something was smashing the end of his long, closed tunnel.

For a long moment Darius stood in the middle of his cave and thought about what to do. For eight hundred, nine hundred, perhaps a thousand years, Darius had not needed to make up his mind about much of anything. Not since he climbed down off the bow of the long slim ship with the square sail and fierce red-bearded warriors who sailed across the grey northern ocean to a vast, new land.

Darius, who was a full size, twenty foot, pointed tail, long nose dragon, had taken the job as the figurehead at the bow of King Eric's ship on the long voyage across the sea. He had not been happy with a dragon's life and wanted to get away. Far too many of his cousins had fallen under the sword of fame-seeking fierce warriors, or to lovesick knights-errant who wanted to win the hand of some country princess. It was not safe to be a dragon in those days. So Darius had signed aboard the Viking ship to find a peaceful place to snooze away his old age. As soon as the ship touched the rocky beach, he climbed down from the bow and trotted away into the forest.

He traveled quite a few days until he settled on a spot for a new home. It was a lovely place—long rolling meadows crisscrossed with clear streams and surrounded by deep forests.

But the worry of being caught unawares by some swordsman remained in Darius' heart, and he felt he must hide underground. So it was here that he had dug his lair.

The trouble was, it was too comfortable down there in Darius' new home—nice big rooms, and water from

a little spring that seeped down through a rock garden he built—not too warm, not too cold. So when Darius pulled the rocks across his tunnel late one afternoon nearly a thousand years ago, he shut away everything in this land as well as the old one he had left behind.

Life was pleasant down in his caves. He had time to sit and think, time to write the history of the dragon family—Cousin Fafnir, who had curled up around a horde of gold, breathing fire, and ended up with a warrior chopping off his head; Grendel finished off by Beowulf; his French cousin, La Gargouille, done in by mistake, though he had never hurt a hair of a maiden's head. And dozens more of his illustrious dragon family.

Between chapters of his book, Darius would eat a few roots that pushed their way down from the trees and bushes above. And he would sleep a lot. A quiet life it was, and cozy. And there was no reason to make up his mind about much of anything, so it was difficult now for him to know what to do about the pounding and thundering noises coming from the end of his tunnel.

As he stood and thought whether or not he should dig deeper or go and see what the noise was, a sudden draft raced through his cave blowing out the candle on his desk and causing him to have a sneezing fit. When he recovered, he heard another deafening thump at the end of the tunnel.

"I must be prepared to fight," said Darius, "for I fear

10

this means some monster is trying to force his way into my home."

From over his fireplace he took down his old jewel-encrusted sword and moved a cold cup of root tea from his ancient brass shield which he had made into a coffee table. He hoisted the shield on one arm and snorted, "Harushchew!" It came out that way because he sneezed right in the middle of a snort.

"I hate drafts. And Swounds, there's a draft in my cave. The first in centuries. I'm being robbed!" he bellowed. "I'll teach that scoundrel, whatever it is—monster, man, or myth—that nothing frightens Darius!" He shouted and began charging up the tunnel. He'd forgotten that he had not been sure of what to do a little earlier. All Darius remembered now was that he was a dragon threatened by something, and no dragon ever ran away.

The draft down the tunnel had now become a roaring wind.

"Intolerable!" shouted Darius.

Looking ahead to the end of the tunnel, he saw something that stopped him in his tracks. It was a shaft of light. He could hardly understand what he was seeing, it had been so long. But it looked like—yes, it was—a large patch of blue sky! Darius was not pleased at seeing it, for it meant one thing to him. Some monster had broken into his hideaway.

And just then he saw it. A great slab-like jaw, with big shiny teeth sticking out in a cruel row along the bottom, slammed against the tunnel, knocking away some more rocks. It bit into the earth so hard that the whole tunnel shook. Some boulders fell out of the roof of the tunnel, striking Darius, knocking him down and dazing him. By the time he'd shaken his head and cleared it enough to see what was happening, a still larger chunk of blue sky showed above him.

"What kind of a monster is this?" thought Darius. "He'll eat me and my cave if I don't stop him." He laid his ears back, fanned his leathery wings with their spikes on the tips, switched his razor-edged tail, dug his claws into the earth and rattled the scales on his silvery hide. Then he lunged forward, swinging his sword, but the monster retreated a few paces and changed position. Darius stepped back too, waiting for a chance to strike a mortal blow.

Then the monster attacked again and took a giant mouthful of earth. Darius jumped aside, without even a chance to swing his sword, just as the teeth were about to strike near his snout. He was sent tumbling down the tunnel with the dirt and rocks. Angered beyond words at the rudeness of his opponent, Darius did something

12

he hadn't done for over nine hundred years. He tried blowing fire, but there was no fire. It had been centuries since he had tried. He resolved he would certainly never again get out of practice. He had forgotten what a useful thing it was. In his youth he had won quite a reputation burning down a number of castles and huge barns. But that was long ago. Darius pulled his old bones together, and while the agility and the fire of youth had long left him, his courage remained, and he set out once again to challenge the growling monster above.

This time he stayed pressed against the side of the tunnel holding on to a tree root with one paw. When the great jaw appeared high above him, Darius swung out with his sword with all his might and sent it crashing with a resounding clang against the monster's teeth. So great was his effort and so ineffective was the blow against the beast, that Darius and his sword were sent spinning down the tunnel once again.

Undaunted Darius climbed back up the tunnel and listened carefully. It seemed to him the monster's growling was suddenly not so loud. Could it be that he had frightened it away? Heartened, he determined to pull himself to the top of the tunnel where he could look out.

Cautiously he made his way up the littered tunnel, cheered because no great jaw loomed above him and no teeth devoured the very earth he was standing on. When he reached the great open hole at the top, he saw a huge, hulking orange beast, smoking and growling, slowly rumble away. Darius was sure the monster was retreating. Across the grass it went. Darius stared in wonder at the beast, for never in his thousands of years had he seen anything so enormous, so ugly, and so formidable.

"He will be back," Darius said to himself, "for I have only wounded him. What shall I do?" He must find the king of this land, he decided, and tell him about the monster at once.

"Surely when the king finds out what his monster has done, he will order him destroyed," he said.

Darius climbed out of the tunnel and looked around him. What a strange kingdom this had become! It didn't look at all the way he remembered. The flower-filled meadows and clear streams were gone. Instead of deep forests, strange buildings were everywhere. Darius thought they seemed too tall to stand alone—and he noticed the streets were full of shiny, honking creatures.

"Odd," thought Darius, as he brushed the dirt from himself and started off in search of the king.

As he moved along, he was aware of noise everywhere. Overhead giant roaring birds barely missed the tops of the tall buildings, and sirens and whistles and all manner of strange sounds alarmed him.

"Screech! Honk! Beep! Honk!"

"Get outa the way, ya dumb—ya dumb—whatever you are!" a man yelled at him.

"Watch out, you!" shouted another.

"Honk, honk, honk! Screech!"

"Can't you kids act and dress like normal human beings?" yelled someone else.

"Kids?" snorted Darius. "What's the matter with these people?"

"Hey, Mister, over here," called a voice.

The confused dragon looked around and saw a young boy motioning to him. But just then a big bus roared by and the exhaust fumes caused Darius to have a coughing spell. "Honk! Honk! Beep! Honk!" the horns blasted at Darius, but his eyes stung and he couldn't see. He felt a tug on his arm; someone was leading him to safety through the tangle of strange, noisy, smelling, smoking, beasts.

Darius wiped his eyes and looked to see who had pulled him from the stampede of strange beasts. There stood the same little boy who had called to him.

"Wow! You almost got hit!" said the boy. "Don't you know you're not supposed to cross the street against the light, and in the middle of the block? Where you from, man?"

But Darius just leaned unsteadily against a post for a few moments, catching his breath.

"You can sit down here," said the boy, indicating some steep steps in front of a tall brown building. "You look all shook up."

Gratefully, Darius sat and the boy let him rest in silence for a few moments.

Presently Darius said, "Thank you, young man. You have saved my life. I am deeply indebted to you."

The boy looked at Darius for a few minutes and then shrugged. "This is my pad," he said.

"I beg your pardon?" asked Darius.

"My pad," said the boy. "I live here."

"Oh?" said Darius, looking up the steep steps to the tall, narrow brown building behind him. He noticed that all the buildings down the street were the same, and each one had steep steps in front of it. "How do you know this one is yours?" asked Darius.

The boy viewed him with wonder. "You're sure dumb," he said.

"Hardly that, young man!" said Darius, somewhat miffed. "All these houses look alike, so I wondered how you could know which is yours. That's all."

"They're not houses, Mister, they're tenements," said the boy. "And I know this is mine—because I live here, that's why."

"Oh," said Darius. He was so tired and confused that he saw no point in pursuing this further.

"How come you look so funny?" asked the boy.

"Do I look funny?" asked Darius, surprised.

"Sort of," said the boy.

"Well, I look like what I am," said the dragon.

16

"What's that?" asked the boy.

"What's what?" asked Darius.

"What you are."

Darius looked at the small boy sitting next to him in amazement. "Why, I am a dragon, of course," he said.

"Oh," said the boy and began playing with a Yo-yo he took out of his pocket.

"Haven't you ever seen a dragon before?" asked Darius.

"Nope," said the boy. He got up and twirled the Yo-yo up and down and over his head and around in a circle.

"It seems to me, young fellow, that you have a very abrupt way of talking to people," Darius said. "And," he added to himself, "it is odd that you don't recognize a dragon."

Suddenly the boy stopped playing with the Yo-yo and walked over to Darius. He put his face down next to his and stared into it hard.

"Where do you live, dragon?" asked the boy.

"Aha! Aha, aha!" said Darius, suddenly remembering why he was there. Leaping to his feet he said, "That's what I've come about, young man. I must find your king at once."

"Huh?" said the boy.

"Your king. I must find your king."

The boy looked at Darius and wrinkled up his nose in a puzzled expression.

"You're sure funny," he said.

"We've been through that before," said Darius, sternly. "Now I must find your king—your emperor—your ruler."

The boy gazed at Darius with a look of contempt. "Man, you are way out."

"Come, come, young man, don't tell me you have no leader," said the dragon.

The boy thought and then shrugged and said that he might know someone like that.

"Excellent!" said the dragon. "Would you be kind enough to take me to his castle?"

The boy laughed. "It ain't no castle, Mister."

"Well, wherever he is, then," said the dragon.

"This is surely a very strange kingdom," Darius thought to himself, "with a king the boy has trouble remembering—and no castle."

"By the way," the dragon said, "my name is Darius." And the dragon bowed his head to the boy.

"Boy, is Louie ever going to be surprised when he sees you," the boy replied.

"Louie?" asked the dragon.

"Yeah," said the boy. "He's our leader."

"Oh," said Darius. "But don't you call him King?"

"Sometimes—just for laughs," said the boy. "And he kind of likes it, too. All that king jazz, I mean."

"Hmm, King Jazz," Darius said to himself. "I must

remember to call him by his proper title. King Jazz."

"Are you a special member of his court?" Darius asked aloud, but got no answer. He tried again. "What do you do there?"

"I'm on one of his teams," the boy said. "Basketball," he added proudly.

"If you are on, uh, his team, does that mean, then, that you are royalty, too?" asked Darius.

"I play forward, sometimes guard," the boy shrugged. "It just depends."

"Forward—guarding?" said Darius to himself.

"Second string," said the boy.

"Then you must be a knight?" said Darius joyfully.

The boy looked up at Darius and scowled.

"I ain't any night," he said, angrily.

"Of course you're not just *any* knight," Darius was quick to answer. "I'm sure you are a special knight—a very brave and courageous one. It's the king's good fortune to have you in his service. I intend to tell him so when I see him."

The boy put his head to one side, whistled soundlessly and studied Darius.

"I once wanted to be a knight," Darius went on, "but that, I'm afraid, was a very long time ago—very long, indeed." And the dragon was lost in thought for a few minutes. "Well, well," he said presently, "should we go, Sir Knight?"

"Don't call me night," the boy said.

"Whatever you say, sir," said Darius. "But what—but what should I call you then?"

"My name," said the boy.

"What is your name, sir?"

"William Grover Jones," the boy announced, speaking loudly and clearly.

"My, my. Three names," said the dragon. "You must be very important."

The boy thought a minute, then shrugged. "Well, I am, sort of," he said.

"Then I'll call you—Sir William. How's that?" asked the dragon.

The boy thought a moment. "OK," he said.

"Oh, by the way," the dragon said uneasily, suddenly remembering something. "You aren't trying to win the hand of some princess, are you?"

The boy gave Darius such a peculiar look that the dragon just muttered, "No, I suppose not," and dismissed it from his mind.

Darius asked the boy where the king held court, and William told him he was usually at the basketball court this time of year, though sometimes at the volleyball court. Darius thought that this king with two courts must certainly be powerful.

When the dragon asked how far it was to the court, William told him it was at the park just a couple of blocks away. The dragon then suggested they get started, for he was very anxious to see the king as soon as possible.

William motioned for the dragon to follow, and he led him down the street.

2

William spent precious time whistling and leaping over trash cans and jumping over cracks in the sidewalk, leapfrogging over fire hydrants and peering down gratings, kicking cans and swinging on fences, so it took them awhile to go the two blocks.

Suddenly the dragon saw something that caused him to stop abruptly. "There it is! There's the monster!" he cried, pointing down the street. He was very excited, and William ran over to him.

"What monster?" he asked.

"*The* monster! The monster that is destroying my home!"

"You mean that old bulldozer?" asked William.

"Yes, yes, that's it! What did you call it?" asked Darius.

"A bulldozer," William said.

"Hmm, ah," said Darius, watching it. "A large bull, you say? A dozer bull? Strange." And he stared at it a moment. "Well, I must hurry and see your king before that monster eats more of my home. Where did you say he was?"

"In the park," said William. "In that building over there." He pointed across the street at a low brick building on the far side of the park.

"Ah," said Darius. "How do we get there?" he asked, looking at the busy street in front of them filled with honking speeding beasts and remembering his near catastrophe before.

"Follow me," said William, going to the corner. "Wait here," he told the dragon. "See that light over there?" He pointed to the traffic light across the street.

"Yes," said Darius.

"Well, when that's green, it means we can walk across," said William.

"But do those wild animals know that?" asked Darius.

"What wild animals?" William asked, looking out into the street where Darius was pointing.

"Those," the dragon said, indicating the rushing cars.

William laughed. "Those aren't wild animals. They're cars."

"Hmph," snorted Darius. "They act like wild animals."

"OK, it's green," said William. "We can go now."

"Come on," said William as Darius hesitated.

"But those cars are going," said Darius, pointing to the traffic on the side street.

"Well, it's their turn. They've got a green light, and these cars on this street have a red, so that means it's green for us."

Darius looked with wonder at the small boy. "I don't understand that at all," he said.

"Come on," said William. "You'll get used to it." And he took hold of Darius and led him across the street to the park.

When they were safely across, Darius sighed with relief. "I'm glad that's over," he said. "Now let's see your king."

As they came nearer to the building, Darius saw that a number of young people near it were playing games, throwing balls through hoops, swinging on swings, and chasing one another. Some of the boys stopped playing when they saw William and Darius approaching.

"Hey—hey, Jones," one called. "Who's that?" he asked, pointing to Darius.

"A friend," said William, walking past without looking at them.

"Some friend," laughed one, and the others joined in.

"Steal him from the zoo?" called another. But William paid no attention.

"Where's Louie?" William asked a boy who was standing near the door. Inside the building they headed toward some big doors at the end of a short hall. A terrible racket was coming from behind the doors.

"It sounds as if they're having some kind of celebration," Darius shouted over the noise to William.

"Naw, it always sounds like that," William said, as he opened the big doors.

"My word," said Darius. The noise that greeted them nearly deafened the poor dragon. Whistles were blowing and people were running and shouting and throwing balls into hoops.

"What are they doing?" asked Darius.

"Playing basketball. This is the basketball court," William said. "There's Louie over there." He pointed to a larger boy who was blowing a whistle on a chain he had around his neck. Darius ducked his head as William led him through the doors into the gym.

"That's the king? This is a court?" asked Darius, surprised. He looked around for signs of a throne but saw none.

"Come on," William said, and they started across the gym to where Louie was standing. Just then Louie looked up and saw them, and the whistle he had been blowing fell from his mouth as he silently gaped at William and his strange-looking new friend. One by one the others in the room turned to look. Presently the only sound to be heard in the once noisy room was William and Darius walking across the polished wooden floor.

When they were in front of Louie, William turned to Darius and said, "Here he is."

"Your Majesty," Darius said, bowing his long neck to Louie. Then he straightened up and said, "Your gallant knight, here, Sir William, who courageously rescued me, was kind enough to bring me here. I would be most grateful, King Jazz, if you were to grant me an audience."

Louie blinked and just stared at the dragon. "What gives with this cat?" he asked William.

William shrugged and said, "He was crossing the street in the middle of the block and I pulled him out. He said he wanted to see you, so I brought him here."

"I would speak with you, King Jazz, about a serious, a pressing problem" said Darius.

"What's the King Jazz bit?" Louie asked William.

"He thinks you're King Jazz," William explained, taking a stick of gum out of his pocket and putting it into his mouth.

"King Jazz?" Louie asked, puzzled.

"Hey, man! King Jazz!" yelled some of the boys. Then all of them whistled and stomped and laughed, all vowing to call Louie King Jazz from then on.

Louie blew his whistle. "Knock it off," he said. Then he turned to William. "What is he?"

"A dragon," William said.

"A *dragon?*" said Louie, and the room became silent. Then one of the boys shouted, "Who says?"

"He says," said William.

"Aw, there ain't no such things as dragons," called another. But when Darius turned and glowered, the boy who had said this grew suddenly very quiet, and no one else in the room made a sound.

"What—what does he want?" asked Louie, after a moment.

"I don't know," said William. "But he's got some kind of problem."

"You can say that again," sniggered one boy and they all laughed.

"Shut up!" Louie yelled at the boys. When it was quiet again, he turned to the dragon and asked, "You—wanted to see me?"

"Yes, sire," said the dragon.

"What about?" asked Louie, trying to keep his voice from showing the fear he felt, because he'd heard stories about dragons.

"Well, Your Majesty," Darius began, but laughter rippled through the room interrupting him. He turned and slowly looked about, squinting his eyes as he did so, which silenced the boys. He cleared his throat loudly and continued.

"Your Majesty," he began again, and this time no one laughed. "This morning while I was working at my desk, I heard a dreadful noise, and then a draft blew through my cave. When I went to see where this disturbance came from, there—at the end of the tunnel to my cave—was a patch of blue sky where none had been before. Your beast, sire, had dug an entrance to my cave."

Darius stopped, looked around, and waited. But no one moved a muscle except to look in silence at one another and back at the dragon. So Darius continued.

"Well, sire, this monster—this dozer bull, as you call him—was devouring my very home, a home I have lived in peacefully for over nine hundred years. Sire, this is an intolerable situation! Not only is my privacy—which I value more than life itself—in grave danger, but now my cave is exceedingly drafty. And I hate drafts!"

Darius stopped and took out a handkerchief and sneezed at the very thought of it. Then he sniffed a few times and went on. "Excuse me, King Jazz, but the mere mention of a draft makes me sneeze." He blew his nose, and Louie looked around at the others and back at the dragon. Then he nodded to Darius; he didn't know what else to do.

"Well, Your Majesty," Darius continued, "I engaged your beast in combat, but I succeeded only in wounding him. I saw him retreating across the grass. But I have no doubt that he will be back, for I saw him lurking about as we were approaching your court. Now I do not know in what esteem Your Majesty, and your kingdom, for that matter, holds the dozer bull. But in my judgment he is a rude, ill-mannered, loudmouthed beast with whom I am quite certain I cannot live in peace! I am a non-violent dragon by nature, sire, but this is too much! I will not have it!" he thundered.

Darius stopped and stared at Louie.

Louie stared back at the dragon, openmouthed, and then swallowing hard, he turned to William and said as quietly as he could, "What's he talking about?"

William shrugged and chewed his gum.

Louie turned back to the dragon and managed a weak smile, but Darius did not change the stern expression which had been on his face since he began talking. Louie licked his lips nervously and whispered hoarsely to William, "What's a dozer bull?"

"A bulldozer," said William.

Louie shifted from one foot to the other and scratched his head.

"Uh—dragon," he began, uncertainly.

"My name is Darius, Your Majesty," the dragon said, bowing his head to Louie.

"Huh?" said Louie. "Oh—Darius. OK. Well, Darius, I don't dig what you're talking about, see?"

He looked at Darius with a puzzled expression. And Darius said, "It's very simple, Your Majesty. Your dozer bull has wrecked my home, and I want to know what you're going to do about it."

Louie stared at the dragon. "Look," he began, "I—"

"Maybe he means the bulldozer wrecked his pad," one boy said.

"Yeah," said another. "They started knocking down that hill at the back of the park. Maybe that's where he lives."

"Yeah, and maybe he turns into a pumpkin at midnight," laughed another.

"That's Cinderella or Red Riding Hood, or something, you dope," said another.

"Yeah, well, who believes in dragons?" yelled someone else.

"Wait a minute! Wait a minute!" Louie called. He thought a minute. "Yeah, maybe that's it. Say, where do you live, dragon—I mean, Darius?"

"Across the green meadow," said Darius.

"He means across the park," William said.

"Oh," said Louie, "then let's look."

So Darius led the boys through the big doors, down the short hall and out of the low brick building. "This way," he called, and everyone who had been in the building and all those who were outside followed him. Everyone, that is, except one or two who claimed they didn't believe in dragons.

When the group reached a large dirt mound, Darius said, "This is it. This, King Jazz, is what your monster dozer bull has done to my home. This was the entrance

31

to my once peaceful life." Darius was so overcome at seeing the ugly gaping hole in what had been his home that a tear dropped from his eye.

The boys thought it was strange for a dragon to cry, but they pretended not to notice. They looked at the overturned earth and saw the mouth to an ancient tunnel, now choked by rocks and debris.

"Yeah," said Louie. "This is the place all right. The bulldozer was working here this morning."

"Well then," said the dragon, now looking more angry than sad, "what are you going to do about it?"

"Huh?" asked Louie.

"Surely, King Jazz, you will have your monster dozer bull destroyed before he does any more damage," said Darius. "Personally, I cannot understand why you would allow such a menace to run loose in the first place."

"It's not my idea," said Louie. "We don't like it any more than you do."

"What do you mean?" asked Darius.

"He means," said one boy, "that we don't want our park torn up either."

"They're tearin' up the only place left for us to play!"

"Do you mean," said Darius, "that this monster doesn't belong to you?"

"That's it, dragon," Louie said.

"Then what's he doing here?" Darius asked.

"He's digging up the park to make a parking lot," said one of the boys.

"A parking lot? What's that?" asked Darius.

Some of the boys laughed and poked each other.

"It's a place for—for those," a boy said, pointing to the cars rushing by in the street.

Darius was appalled. "Swounds!" he said. "Why, that's dreadful! This place has gone mad!"

"Yeah, we don't think it's so hot ourselves," said Louie.

"But you're the king," Darius said to Louie. "Surely, you can order the monster destroyed."

Everyone laughed at this.

"Yeah, well, maybe I'm the king around here, man, but that doesn't mean anything out there," Louie laughed, nodding toward the buildings in the background.

Darius looked at Louie with a puzzled expression, and then he put his head to one side and thought for a moment. "Do you mean that this is your kingdom," he said, pointing to the park, "and that out there is another kingdom?"

"Well," Louie said, scratching his head. "I guess you could say that. I mean, it's a different sort of place, and that's for sure."

"So this is the Kingdom of Park," Darius said, "and the dozer bull is not yours. Hmm." He thought for a minute. "Well, which kingdom owns the dozer bull?"

Louie shrugged and said, "They do."

"Yes, but who are *they?*" asked the dragon, becoming a bit impatient.

"I don't know. I suppose you could call them the—the Establishment, or something," Louie said.

"The Establishment?" asked Darius.

"Man, you sure ask nutty questions," said Louie.

"Then—then your Kingdom of Park is being invaded by the Kingdom of Establishment," said Darius, pacing back and forth.

"Huh?" said Louie.

"Well, what are you doing about it?" demanded Darius, stopping abruptly and facing Louie.

"About what?" asked Louie.

"The invasion!" Darius snapped.

Louie looked blankly at him a minute, and then he muttered under his breath to William. "You really did it, kid," he said. "This guy's a real nut."

"King Jazz," Darius repeated sternly, "what are you doing about the invasion?"

"I don't know," said Louie, looking around helplessly. "Nothing, I guess."

"Nothing?" shouted Darius. "What kind of king are you anyway? Here your very kingdom, your lovely grassy homeland, is being invaded and destroyed by a monster dozer bull, and you do *nothing?*"

"Look, I don't think you get it, dragon. I mean, it's

kind of complicated," Louie said, hoping to end the discussion, or at least change the subject.

"How?" asked Darius.

Louie looked at the dragon and shook his head and sighed. "Well—like when they say there's going to be a parking lot instead of a park," he said, "well—like that's the way it is. See?"

Darius looked at Louie for a long moment. "Hmph," Darius snorted. "You'll pardon me, King Jazz, if I tell you that I don't think you're much of a king."

"I suppose not," said Louie, looking a bit embarrassed.

"But he sure knows how to play basketball," volunteered one boy.

"All well and good," snorted Darius. "And when your Kingdom of Park is gone, where will you play?"

The boy shrugged. Darius looked long and hard at King Jazz and his ragtag royal court, and began pacing back and forth, muttering to himself. Every now and then he would stop and look at the group, shake his head in amazement, and start pacing again.

"Uh, we did have a demonstration once," said Louie.

"Yeah, we did!" said the others, hoping to please the angry dragon. "We had signs about not making the park into a parking lot."

"It didn't do any good, though," said another.

"And what, may I ask, is a demonstration?" demanded Darius.

35

"Well, it's a sort of protest," explained Louie. But the dragon just stared at him. "It's a—well, everybody gets signs and—and has a kind of parade, see?"

Darius brightened. "Is it like a crusade?" he asked, excitedly. Louie and the others looked at each other. But before they could answer, Darius was pacing very fast and saying "A crusade. Of course, of course. Brilliant idea, oh, King! But you must have another crusade! And I will lead it! Many members of my family were in crusades. Oh, in my day, my friends, I could have led many of them! I might add, I would have cut a brilliant figure in that role. Ah, there is nothing—nothing, my friends, like a good crusade! Oh, I can feel my blood running. Heh, heh." And Darius leaped and fenced and charged about the park while the bewildered group of boys stood watching and wondering.

Presently the dragon came over to the boys and sat down. He was out of breath from so much running about.

"Ho hum!" sighed Darius. "Just a bit out of condition. I tell you what," he puffed, "while I sit here catching my breath, you, King Jazz, and your court assemble your battle equipment and get your banners. We will meet here. We'll begin our crusade immediately!"

3

"Are we gonna have another demonstration now?"
William asked Louie.

"I guess so," said Louie, uncertainly.

"Oh, boy!" yelled one boy. Then the others joined in
and all jumped about joyously. "I'm going to go get my
signs," said one, and the others followed his suggestion
and ran off to get theirs.

"Well, I guess it's OK—but it didn't do much good,"
said Louie, and left to get his.

William didn't leave. He stood looking down at the
winded dragon. Darius had shut his eyes, and had begun
to doze, when William sat down next to him and tugged
at his elbow.

"Hey, Mister Dragon," said William.

"Hump, hm—what?!" said Darius, awakening from
his too short nap. "What are you doing here? Why

aren't you off with the others getting your signs?" Darius asked.

"I just want to know something," William said.

"Well?" said Darius, somewhat cross at being awakened. "Well? Speak up!"

"Well," William said quietly, "I just wondered if you were a real dragon, that's all."

Darius stared at him scornfully. "Ods Bodkins! I am a real dragon and that's an end to it. Why?"

"Because," William began, "because a lot of things aren't real. I mean, people say things but sometimes it ain't so. They say they're gonna do something, and they don't. I found you, so I got to know if you're real or if you're just saying things and not meaning them."

"Well, I am real!" said Darius, "You may be sure of that. But I am also a very tired dragon, and I would like to have a little nap—if you don't mind," he added, sarcastically.

"Oh, I don't mind," said William, not moving.

The dragon tried to sleep, but William's presence disturbed him. "Young man, I'm used to my privacy. Just you run along with the others for a while, all right?"

"But you might go away," said William.

"Go away? Go away where?" asked the dragon.

"Just away," said William.

"Look here, Sir William, don't you trust me?" asked the dragon.

"I don't trust much of nobody or nothin'," said William.

"Well, you should change that," said Darius. "It's very bad for you." And he began to doze again.

William sat quietly observing the resting dragon for a few moments. He reached out and lightly touched his wing, and then put his head down next to the dragon's nose and looked at it. Darius awoke with a start to stare directly into the eyes of William. He jumped.

"Great Valhalla!" cried the dragon. "Now what?"

"I was just looking at your nose," said William.

"What's wrong with my nose?" asked Darius.

"Nothing, I guess," said William.

"Well, I am glad to hear you say that," retorted the dragon crossly. "And now since you've found there's nothing wrong with my nose, do you suppose it would be all right if I continued my nap—uninterrupted?"

William shrugged. "It's OK with me," he said, and he began drawing pictures in the dirt with a stick.

Darius muttered to himself as he tried to find a comfortable position. Just as he had settled down again, William said, "Real dragons blow fire out of their noses."

"What? What's that?" said Darius, now quite angry and just a bit unsettled by this statement.

"I said real dragons blow fire out of their noses," repeated William. "Like this one," he said, indicating to

Darius the small picture he had drawn in the dirt.

"What's that supposed to be?" said Darius, looking at the picture.

"It's a dragon. See? This is the fire coming out of its nose."

"Hmph," said Darius, "that doesn't look very good to me. Looks more like an elephant than a dragon."

"Oh, it's a dragon, all right," said William. "A *real* one."

"See here, young man, are you telling me that I am not a real dragon?" said Darius.

William shrugged. "I'm just saying that real dragons can blow fire out of their noses. That's all."

"And so, if I'm a real dragon, I should be able to blow fire out of my nose. Is that right?" asked Darius. He reflected that in his youth he would have stepped on anyone who talked like this and flattened him fast.

William shrugged and went on drawing.

"And what if I told you that I'm too old for all that fire blowing, and that I'm completely out of practice."

"I don't care," William shrugged, not looking up.

"But you won't believe I'm real unless I blow fire. Is that it?" asked Darius.

William nodded and continued to draw.

"I see," said Darius. And he looked at the small boy beside him and suddenly he wished with all his old heart that he could blow fire.

He was sitting wondering how he could explain his problems to one so young when the boys began shouting and running across the grass with their signs.

"Here they come!" Darius said. He became very excited again at the thought of a crusade, and for a few moments he felt like a young dragon again.

"Come along, come along!" Darius shouted.

Soon all the boys had arrived and Darius examined their handmade signs.

"Excellent," he said as he looked at the signs that came in all colors and all sizes and said things such as WE WANT OUR PARK, WE CAN'T PLAY BALL IN PARKING LOTS, HELP SAVE OUR PARK, GREEN GRASS AND TREES NOT CONCRETE, CHILDREN NEED PARKS, KIDS NOT CARS.

"Excellent, excellent," said the dragon.

"Now then, King Jazz, you will follow me," said Darius. "I mean no disrespect to royalty, sire, but I have always wanted to lead a crusade and so I feel quite compelled to lead this one. I have quite a stake in it, too, you know."

If the truth be known, Darius could hardly wait. Louie shrugged and said it was all right with him.

Darius began shouting orders and the boys formed a line behind Louie. Just then several boys and girls came running across the park with bongo drums, kazoos, musical combs, washboards and various other homemade instruments.

"I hear you're having a demonstration," one said.

"We are having a crusade," said Darius.

The newcomers looked puzzled.

"It's sort of the same thing, I guess," Louie explained to them.

"Can we come, too?" they asked.

"Who are these people, sire? Are they your wandering minstrels?" Darius asked.

"In a way, yeah," said Louie.

"Very well, come then, minstrels," said Darius, "get in line, and when I give the signal to march, you may begin playing."

Darius stood back to look at the little band of young people and he smiled approvingly. "Oh, excellent!" he said. "This will be a fine crusade."

"But wait," he said, frowning. "We have no colors."

"We've got all kinds of colors," said one boy, pointing to the many different colored signs, people, and clothes making up the group.

"Not that kind," said Darius. "King Jazz, we must have some colors—some special sign to identify us. We can't have a proper crusade without one."

"Now what," grumbled one boy, anxious to start.

"Of course!" shouted Darius, pointing to a bush that had been run over by the bulldozer. "Take up the fallen colors!" he called, taking a branch of green leaves from the ground and presenting it to Louie. "Your

Majesty, your crusade colors," said Darius, bowing low.

A few newcomers sniggered at this, but Darius gave them such a fearful look, they stopped abruptly.

Darius picked up a branch for himself and placed it on top of his head between his ears. The others picked up branches and stuck them in their caps or in their hair.

"Now then, sire, if you are ready, we shall begin."

Louie nodded, and Darius gave the signal to the minstrels to begin playing.

"Aren't you coming?" Darius said to William, who was still sitting on the ground drawing in the dust.

"I guess," he shrugged, and joined the group.

"Onward!" shouted Darius, and off they went, tooting and shouting and drumming back and forth and all around the park.

Some traffic on the streets slowed down to watch and soon horns were honking, whistles blowing, and tempers exploding, but those in the crusade did not notice. They were too busy trying to keep up with Darius. He was bounding about the park, shouting and waving his banner and slashing the air with his sword. It was such a fine performance that those who were following him would gladly have stopped in order to watch.

A policeman came by to investigate the noise. He stopped short when he saw what was causing the commotion.

"What is that?" he said, seeing the dragon. "Just look at them kids. They'll wear anything these days! I'd better call the chief. Looks like some kind of riot to me." With that he hurried off to a police phone so he could report to headquarters.

Darius was slashing at the air when he suddenly stopped and held up a paw for silence among the crusaders. He listened, concerned.

He thought he had heard the low growling sound of the beast, and now he was sure of it. He looked across the park and there the bulldozer was, lumbering determinedly toward the hole it had begun that morning.

"There it is!" cried Darius. "There is the dozer bull from the Kingdom of Establishment." And he turned to his followers and said, "Stand fast. This is a dragon's work." And with that he rushed toward the bulldozer, brandishing his sword menacingly. Then he stopped. "Ho," he said, "I will take the beast by surprise," and he hopped down into the entrance to his cave and waited.

Just as the bulldozer reached the hole, Darius attacked it. "Clang, cling, clunk," went his sword as it slashed harmlessly across the giant jaw of the great beast.

The sleepy driver, who had just finished his lunch break, did not notice that his bulldozer was being attacked by a dragon. He brought the blade up to such a position that Darius could not see where it was because of the sun shining in his eyes. The driver yawned, turned the machine toward the hole, and started lowering the steel blade on the very spot where Darius was defiantly standing his ground.

"Watch out! Watch out!" William cried, rushing toward the dragon and pushing him out of the way. He pushed Darius with such force that both he and the dragon went sprawling into the dirt at the side of the hole.

At that moment the steel blade came down with a loud thud on the very spot where Darius had been standing and greedily gobbled a mouthful of dirt and fresh grass and yellow flowers.

"Monster!" shouted Darius, getting to his feet. But just then the bulldozer released its load of earth, covering Darius and William.

4

Darius sputtered and fumed and made his way out of the dirt and began looking for William. He found him underneath the dirt, crying.

"Here, here," said Darius. "You are a brave and gallant knight. You mustn't cry. And I thank you, sir, for again coming to my rescue."

William hugged the dragon. "I'm afraid," he cried. "I'm afraid you'll get hurt." The dragon was very touched. He could not remember anyone ever caring what happened to him before.

Thinking William had been hurt, the young people rushed at the bulldozer, shouting and waving their signs ominously. Several picked up clods of dirt and threw them at the machine.

"Hey!" said the driver, as he saw the youngsters and heard the earth clumps thud against the bulldozer.

"Hey! What's going on? Get away from here before you get hurt!"

"That's right," shouted Darius. He told William to join the rest. "Now, King Jazz, order your troops to stand back. I don't want anyone hurt. When I need you I'll give the command."

Darius raised his sword and began what could only be described as a few minutes of brilliant dueling with the dozer bull.

"Clink, slash, clunk, swish," went Darius's sword.

The young people cheered as Darius parried and thrust with great skill and grace, considering his age and size.

"Hey, he's OK," said Louie, admiringly.

The bulldozer driver looked to see what everyone was cheering about. Just as he peered over the front, Darius glared up into the face of the startled driver.

"Yeowk," cried the driver seeing the dragon's face glowering into his. He leaped from the bulldozer. "You can't hit my bulldozer," he cried. "Hey!" But Darius continued slashing at the bulldozer with his sword.

"I'm gonna get my boss," cried the driver, running across the park as fast as he could. "Help! We're being invaded by monsters!" he yelled. "Get the police! Get the mayor! Get the sheriff! Get *somebody!*"

While Darius continued to attack the bulldozer, the police chief drove up accompanied by Finley, the officer who had phoned him.

"There, sir," cried Finley, pointing to the park. "Over there, by the bulldozer."

The police chief, who was quite nearsighted, had some trouble locating the park.

"What do you see?" he asked Finley.

"Well, sir, why—why that fellow, whoever he is, is waving a sword and hitting the bulldozer with it," Finley said.

"Great scott! Why that's city property!"

"Yes sir," said Finley, pleased. "I figured I ought to call you, sir."

Just then the frightened bulldozer driver ran by, yelling about monsters.

"Well, well," said the chief. "Attacking city property and frightening our citizens."

"I thought you ought to know, sir," said Finley, beaming.

"Yes, yes, Finley, you said that," said the chief. "Well?"

"Well, what, sir?" answered Finley.

"Well, arrest him!" the chief shouted.

Finley gulped. "Me, sir?"

"Of course! Can't you see he is destroying city property?"

Finley peered out of the police car and looked at the dragon, still slashing at the bulldozer.

"Yeah," said Finley.

"Well, do something!" yelled the chief.

"What?" said Finley.

"Well, what does your book say to do!" said the chief through gritted teeth. "Under Section A—Willfully destroying city property. Well, Finley?" Finley stared blankly at the chief.

"Finley, don't you remember anything?" the chief groaned.

"Yes, sir," said Finley, taking out his police manual and thumbing through it.

"Not now, you idiot," yelled the chief. "Go arrest him!"

As Finley hesitated, the chief grew impatient.

"Never mind," he said. "I'll do it myself." He got out of the police car and Finley pointed out the way to him.

"Come along, Finley. Maybe you'll learn something." The chief, followed by Finley, marched off across the grass toward Darius and the group of young people.

Just then the empty bulldozer gave a shudder and a low whine, puffed once or twice, then was still.

"Hooray!" shouted the youngsters. And Darius bowed low to them.

"I'm afraid, sire," said the dragon, mopping his

brow, "that the dozer bull is more powerful than we thought. But I think I have succeeded in temporarily stunning him." And another cheer went up. The exhausted Darius sat down in the hole to catch his breath and promptly dozed off.

Suddenly one of the boys looked around and saw the police chief and Finley striding toward them.

"Hey, look!" the boy called.

When the young people saw what was coming, they ran in all directions.

"What's the matter?" asked Louie, looking around.

"Aw, not now," said Louie when he saw the police.

Louie and William and several boys quickly huddled in front of Darius to hide him from the police.

The chief walked up to them and squinted at Louie. "Why, is that you, Louie? *You?*"

"Yes sir," Louie said, miserably.

"What's the meaning of this?" asked the chief.

"Meaning of what?" said Louie.

"Now, Louie, what's going on here?" said the chief.

"Just a little demonstration, chief—you know, save the park, keep the city green, stuff like that."

"Yeah, just a friendly demonstration," added one of the boys who had stayed. He smiled broadly at the police chief.

The chief turned to Finley and barked, "I thought you said someone was hitting a bulldozer!"

"Well, someone, or some*thing* was," said Finley.

The chief turned to Louie. "Was someone hitting a bulldozer around here?" he asked. The boys looked in wonder at one another.

The chief squinted over at the bulldozer. "It looks all right to me. What's the matter with you, Finley?"

"Well, sir, I thought I saw . . ."

"You *thought* you saw *what?*" the chief demanded.

"Well, sir, I thought I saw something—a big silvery something with wings—waving a sword and hitting that bulldozer," Finley said.

The chief stared coldly at Finley for a moment. "How long have you been on the force, Finley?"

"Awhile, sir. I don't know."

"And how many times have you seen some big silvery something with wings whacking a bulldozer with a sword?"

"Well, never, sir—before, I mean," said Finley.

"Great scott, Finley," the chief thundered, "here I am within six weeks of retirement, and you come up with this idiotic story and bring me clear out here to see a bunch of kids parading around with signs. Now, let's go."

About that time Darius awoke from his short nap, raised up, looked around, and said, "What's the matter? Where did everyone go? We haven't finished our crusade yet."

William and Louie tried to motion him back down,

but Darius put his sword into its scabbard and climbed out of the hole.

Finley turned around as Darius was standing up. "Chief! Chief!" he said, tapping the police chief frantically on the shoulder. "Look!"

"Now, what is it?" the chief said, turning.

Finley said nothing, but continued pointing at the dragon.

"Who is that?" asked the police chief, squinting at Darius.

"He's my friend," said William, rushing to the dragon's side.

"Ah, is that your army, King Jazz?" Darius asked, seeing the similar blue uniforms on the two men.

"Uh, well, not exactly," said Louie.

"He's the one, Chief," Finley whispered to his chief.

"What one?" asked the chief.

"The one who was hitting the bulldozer," Finley said, retiring quickly behind the chief, safely away from the dragon.

"Oh, yes," said the chief, walking over to Darius. "So you're the one my officer says was destroying city property."

"He's—he's new around here," William said.

The chief looked at Darius more closely. "I didn't think I recognized him."

"No—no, you don't," Louie said.

"What's your name, son?" the chief asked Darius.

Darius looked down at the chief a moment and then he turned to Louie.

"Who is this?" Darius demanded.

"The police chief," Louie said, and his voice cracked.

Darius looked around and saw some of the young people peering from behind trees throughout the park. "Why is everyone hiding?" he asked. Then he thought a minute. "Hm," he said, "if these men are not your army, are they the army of the Kingdom of Establishment?"

Louie managed a little sick grin and shrugged. "Well, I guess you could say that."

"What's he talking about?" the chief asked Louie.

"Well, he kind of talks funny," Louie explained.

"All kids do," grumbled the chief.

"It takes awhile to get the hang of it," Louie added.

"See here, son," said the chief, squinting up at the dragon. "My, he's a big fellow, isn't he?" he interrupted himself. "I suppose he's on your basketball team?" he asked Louie.

"Well, he could be," said Louie, nodding pleasantly to the chief.

"Yes. Well, he's big enough," said the chief. "But see here, son," he said to the dragon, "whatever made you want to hit a bulldozer?"

"Aha!" Darius bellowed. "So! Is this your dozer bull?"

The boys motioned frantically to Darius not to say anything more. The chief looked puzzled and turned to Louie.

"He means bulldozer," Louie explained.

"Well, yes, in a way," said the chief. "I suppose you could say it's mine. That is, it's the city's. The bulldozer belongs to the city, you see—and we—wait a minute!" he thundered. "I'll ask the questions around here!"

"So, you have come from the Kingdom of Establishment to protect the dozer bull," said Darius. "Stand back, Sir William," Darius said. "King Jazz, order your men to withdraw."

"I don't know," said the police chief, shaking his head sadly, "the older I get, the less I understand you kids."

"I'll handle this myself," said Darius, and he strode up to the police chief.

"On guard, sir!" shouted Darius. And he took a stance and drew his sword and held it in the air in front of the chief. Everyone's mouth dropped open including the chief's, and everyone stared at Darius in disbelief.

Louis put his hands to his forehead and shook his head sadly. "You blew it, dragon," he groaned. "You blew it."

When the surprised chief recovered, he turned to Finley. "Sergeant!" the chief bellowed. "Arrest this man!"

5

"He's not a man," William cried, rushing up to the chief. "He's a dragon, and he doesn't know what he's doing."

"Of course I know what I'm doing," Darius roared.

"Of course he knows what he's doing," the chief echoed. "You see? He agrees with me." And then he stopped and blinked. "Did you say a dragon?" he asked William.

"Yes," William said.

The chief walked up to Darius and looked at him closely.

"By george, I think you're right," he said, after a closer inspection.

"I told you so, chief. I told you," said Finley.

"Yes, yes, Finley," said the chief, who continued to

stare at Darius. "Well, what do you know! A dragon. Now, that is something."

"He's the one who was hitting the bulldozer," Finley whispered urgently to the chief.

"He what? Oh, yes," said the chief, remembering. And seeing Darius' sword, the chief's face grew very stern. "Yes, indeed. Well, we'll have to arrest him," he told Finley.

"Yes sir, that's what I thought," said Finley, staying behind the chief.

"What are they talking about?" Darius asked Louie. But Louie only shook his head miserably.

"We're going to have to take you in, dragon," said the chief. "Section A—Destroying city property. Section C—Carrying a dangerous weapon, and Section . . ."

"But—but he's a dragon," cried William. "And that 's different."

"Always some excuse, eh, Finley?" the chief said. "Still, you may have a point, young man," he said, looking at the dragon. "That could cause a problem."

The chief thought a minute. "Look up dragons, Finley, and see if they're allowed on city streets."

"Yes sir," Finley said, taking out his police manual and flipping through it. "Dragons, dragons," he muttered to himself. "Let's see now, uh, A—B—C . . ."

"Are you going to fight, or aren't you?" Darius said impatiently to the chief.

"What? Never mind, Finley," the chief exploded. "Forget the manual. "I don't care *what* he is. We're taking him in. *Now!* Put the cuffs on him!"

"Me, sir?" Finley quaked.

"Certainly!" roared the chief.

"Yes sir," Finley said, approaching Darius with caution.

"Stand back!" ordered the dragon, waving his sword at Finley.

Finley rushed back to the chief.

"I'm warning you, dragon," said the chief. "If you don't want to get your friends here in trouble, you'll come along peacefully with us."

Darius looked at Louie and William and the others. "I don't understand," he said. "Is this true, King Jazz? Will you be in trouble if I don't go with them?"

Louie nodded.

Darius looked around at the young people who were watching, and Darius said to the chief, "This is certainly very strange. Very well, then, I'll go." And he turned to the chief and said, "I want to speak to your king anyway."

The chief motioned to Finley who held up the handcuffs to Darius and said he would like it very much if he could put them on him. Would he be kind enough to hold out his paw?

Darius thought the silver bracelets must be some kind

of gift, and as he did not wish to appear rude, he held out his paw.

Finley quickly snapped one of the bracelets around the dragon's wrist and then he snapped the other around his own. But he was clearly not happy with this arrangement and stood as far from the dragon as the cuffs would allow.

"Where are we going?" Darius asked the chief.

"Down to City Hall," the chief said.

"Is that where your king is?" asked Darius.

The chief looked at Darius and then at Louie and then at William.

"The mayor—I guess he means," Louie said.

"Yeah, the mayor's there," the chief said to Darius. "Why?"

"Because I must see him on important business," Darius said.

The chief shook his head and muttered something about the fact that he had only six more weeks before he retired and it couldn't come soon enough to suit him. "Come on," he said to Finley.

William looked at Darius handcuffed to Finley and his lower lip trembled.

"Come, come, Sir William," Darius said. "What is the matter?"

"Our crusade is not over," Darius told the solemn little group of friends who were watching with long, unhappy faces. "This way, you see, I shall be able to meet King Mayor of Establishment in person and tell him to destroy his dozer bull so that the Kingdom of Park, and my home, will be safe for me—and for you."

The young people brightened a little and managed a small cheer.

"Enough of that," ordered the chief, who was angry because he hadn't the vaguest idea what the dragon was talking about. "Finley, will you come along?"

"Yes sir," said Finley, giving a slight little tug to Darius with his handcuffed wrist. But the dragon was thinking about meeting a king at City Hall, and at that very moment decided to put away his sword. It was not proper, the dragon felt, to meet a king, no matter what kind of a king it was, with one's sword showing. So just as Finley pulled one way, the dragon swept his arm up and around replacing his sword in its scabbard. This threw Finley completely off balance and he flew through the air in a circle and landed in a dirt heap in front of Darius.

The young people laughed at this and the chief was furious.

"What's the matter with you, Finley?" he bellowed. "Can't you do anything right?" But he soon calmed down when he saw Darius help Finley to his feet and even brush the dirt from his uniform.

"Well, come along. We don't want any more people

watching this performance than we already have." Then he was struck by a sudden thought. "Oohh, if the newspapers hear of this. And television. Good-bye retirement. Let's get him out of here."

"I'll be back before long," the dragon said to his friends. And then he walked across the big park with the chief on one side of him and Finley on the other.

William sat down on the ground and covered his face with his hands and sniffled a couple of times.

"What's the matter now?" asked Louie.

"He hates cars," William said.

And everybody looked across the park at Darius and the police. There certainly did seem to be some trouble when they tried to get Darius into the police car.

But as they looked, the chief talked to the dragon, and soon the dragon calmed down and nodded and managed to put his front feet into the back seat of the police car.

"He won't fit," William moaned.

And he didn't. They had to leave both of the police car's back doors open so the dragon's long neck could stick out on one side, and his long tail on the other. When Darius was finally in, the police car started its siren to clear the streets so it could get through with its wide load.

"He's going to be scared," William cried and ran away from the others and hid behind some bushes.

"Well," said Louie, after the police car was out of sight and they couldn't hear the siren any longer, "anybody want to play basketball, or anything?"

But nobody wanted to and everyone slowly wandered away looking unhappy.

By the time the police car arrived at City Hall, Darius was so shaken that it was no problem at all to lead him quietly through a back door into the jail and lock him in an empty cell. Try as he could, Darius couldn't understand all this, so he simply sat with his eyes shut, slumped against the wall, completely filling the cell.

Word spread quickly around City Hall that there was a dragon in the jail. A number of officials, high and low, made excuses to come toptoeing and whispering past his cell. The mayor himself canceled all his appointments for the afternoon so he could attend to what he referred to as "this little emergency."

"Did you phone the zoo?" the chief whispered to the mayor after they had tiptoed to the cell and were looking in at Darius.

"Yes," said the mayor, "and they don't want him."

"Why not?" asked the chief.

"Too big," replied the mayor. "They said dragons are

troublemakers. And anyway they don't handle extinct animals."

The chief nodded. "Troublemakers—that they are," he agreed. "Well, we've got to do something with him. He can't stay here."

"Of course not!" snapped the mayor. "Terrible publicity. I can't have a dragon in my jail during an election year."

"Sh," said the chief, "you don't want to wake him up. He can be a handful, I'll tell you."

"Well, we've got to get rid of him before the whole town hears about this," whispered the mayor. "We've got an image to think about, you know," he added. And the mayor and the chief stood looking thoughtfully at Darius. Soon the chief was grinning.

"He calls you the king," he said.

"He does?" responded the mayor. "He does—well, well," And then he studied Darius again. "You know," he said, "he looks like a very intelligent creature to me. Yes, very intelligent."

"Yup. Said he wanted to talk to the king," the chief said. "Only way we could get him here was to tell him he could talk to you."

"Is that right?" said the mayor, obviously delighted. But then all at once his expression changed. "I can't talk to a dragon," he worried aloud. "Why, if the press ever got wind of that, I'd never hear the last of it. No. It would never do. Now we've got to think of some way we can get rid of this beast before we become the laughing stock of the whole country."

The chief nodded, thinking of his own retirement. The two men stood looking at Darius and thinking.

6

William, who had hidden unhappily behind some bushes after the police took Darius away, soon decided he was not doing his friend any good that way. He would have to visit him in the jail. He went home and took a jar of peanut butter, a box of corn flakes, and two bananas from a cupboard. Then he hurried off to find City Hall.

When William finally found City Hall, it was much larger than he had expected, and his heart sank to think of his friend lost somewhere in that great building. But because he was not very big, and everyone else was busy talking about the dragon, William had no trouble at all slipping through the halls. He went around corners and through offices, and finally he came to the jail.

The policemen there were so busy running back and forth with stacks of papers in their hands, answering phones, and stopping to whisper in little groups in front of big grey filing cabinets, that William easily slipped inside. Crouching low, he made his way past a tall wooden desk, around another corner, and down a long dark hall. It was dark and there were jail cells on either side of the hall, and the little window at the end had black steel bars across it. William shuddered. "Darius won't like this place," he said.

William crept silently down another little hall and discovered quite suddenly that he was in front of Darius' cell. No one was around. "Hey, pst, Darius," William whispered, but Darius didn't move or open his eyes. William looked at him carefully and saw that he was breathing very heavily. "I guess he's asleep," thought William.

Deciding that he'd try later to waken Darius, William found a dark corner behind a large trash barrel and hid there. He ate some of the corn flakes and part of a banana he had brought and before long, William was fast asleep behind the trash can.

As the police chief followed the mayor into the mayor's office, he stopped suddenly. "Mayor," he began politely, "What about the state park?"

"What about it?" asked the mayor, a round ruddy little man. He plopped down in the swivel chair behind his desk, sighed heavily, and gazed out of his window at the city beyond.

"Well, I thought that might be a good place to send the dragon," said the chief, sitting down in the chair in front of the mayor's desk. But the mayor wasn't listening.

"All those people out there trust me," said the mayor, pointing proudly out the window. "What would they think if they knew we had a dragon in City Hall that we didn't know what to do with? They'd laugh, that's what they'd do. And what would that do to me in an election year? I tell you, it's bad business." And the mayor looked back out the window.

The chief nodded. "Emma and I—that's the wife— we always like to camp there. Got lots of wild animals— raccoons and deer and things like that."

The mayor turned his chair around and studied the chief a moment. "What?" he said.

"Of course, it doesn't have any dragons," the chief continued, "but . . ."

"What are you talking about?" asked the mayor.

"The state park. Great place for a dragon."

The mayor stared at the chief a minute. "The state park," he said. "Of course! It's over three hundred miles from here. Why didn't we think of that sooner? I'll call the governor right now," he said and reached for the phone.

But the governor told the mayor he didn't want any dragons in his state park, and he reminded the mayor that the governor was an elected officer, too.

The police chief said if a state park wouldn't work, maybe a national park would take him. And the mayor said he would call Washington at once and find out.

"After all," chortled the mayor, "I'm not without some influence there." He dialed Washington and asked to speak to several congressmen and senators. But they were out, or busy, or off to Paris or Rome on fact-finding missions, so the only person the mayor could talk to in Washington was the secretary of a newly elected congressman from a remote part of Alaska. She told the mayor she was sure no one in Alaska would vote for a dragon, but she thanked the mayor for his interest anyway.

The mayor hung up and sat staring at the phone with a bewildered expression on his face.

"Why don't you just call Yellowstone direct," said the chief. "We'd better figure out something pretty soon, because I can't find anything in my book about dragons. I don't think we can keep him here much longer—legally, I mean. And if he gets himself a good lawyer, well . . ."

The mayor hurriedly dialed Yellowstone National Park. A tour guide answered the phone. When the mayor told him he had a dragon they might like, the tour guide said the park director and his staff were away on a vacation, but speaking for himself, he would personally like to see a dragon in the park. It would be a great thing. He was getting very tired of nothing but bears, bears, bears.

The mayor was delighted and promised they'd get the dragon to Yellowstone the next day.

"Come on, Chief," he said, "let's go see how we can get that dragon out of here and on his way to Yellowstone tonight."

"Still asleep, eh," the chief said, squinting at Darius between the bars of the cell.

"Yes, and let's hope he stays that way until he's well on his way to Yellowstone," remarked the mayor.

Their voices woke William, who carefully raised himself high enough so he could see over the top of the trash can. He ate the rest of the banana while he listened and watched.

"We'd better measure him so we'll know what size truck we need," said the mayor.

"Right," said the chief. "I'll get Finley." And he walked to the big doors and motioned Finley over.

"You—you wanted me, chief?" said Finley, who had not yet recovered from being handcuffed to a dragon.

"Yes, Finley," said the chief. "Measure the dragon."

"Measure the dragon?" gasped Finley, turning very pale.

"That's right," answered the chief.

Finley turned to the mayor.

"Measure the dragon?" he repeated.

"That's right," said the mayor.

Finley disappeared for a few moments and returned with a yardstick. But he just stood holding it and looking at the dragon.

"Well?" said the chief.

"Well, sir," Finley said, "I don't know how. I've never measured a dragon before."

"Of course not," said the chief, "but that shouldn't stop you."

Finley looked up and the mayor and the chief were staring very hard at him. "Measure a dragon," he muttered to himself, as he approached Darius' cell. "I knew I should have joined the fire department."

Finley poked the yardstick between the bars of the cell and started measuring Darius' tail. But as it was curled around several times, it was difficult for Finley to remember where he had measured. He gave up on the tail and cautiously approached the bars outside the dragon's head and long neck.

71

As he poked through to measure Darius' long neck, the tip of the yardstick touched Darius on the wing, and he let out a snort and shifted his position. Unnerved, Finley fainted dead away on the floor.

William, who had been enjoying this, laughed aloud.

"What was that?" said the chief, squinting in the direction of the trash can.

At that moment Finley moaned, and the chief said, "Get up, Finley. Remember what you are!"

"Yes sir," he replied, and staggered over to the dragon's cell. This time Finley began measuring the cell itself because the dragon surely filled it. He decided he'd add some numbers to it for the tail that was curled around several times, and if he did it all fast enough, and added loudly enough, the mayor and the chief would think he knew what he was doing.

He whipped about, measuring first up, then down, then diagonally this way and that, and all the while saying sums out loud as fast as he could. His performance so impressed the chief and the mayor that when he finished and said the number was two thousand one hundred and twenty three, neither the chief nor the mayor had a question about it. They just slapped him on the back and told him how smart he was.

Finley beamed and started to go.

"Finley, get us a truck to fit that number—and quickly," said the mayor.

"Ahh, sir," said the chief, "Finley works for the police department. I'd like to keep control of my men if I may, sir. Discipline, you know."

"Oh, quite so, quite so," muttered the mayor.

"Finley," said the chief, "get us a truck to—uh—to fit that number."

Finley saluted both men smartly and ran, happy to be escaping from Darius. But the chief called to him. "Not so fast, Finley. I haven't finished."

Finley, who had already trotted halfway down a hall and around a corner, slowly returned and poked his head around the big doors.

"Yes sir?" he answered sadly.

"Then when you get the truck," continued the chief, "bring it back here."

Finley waited a moment and then said, "Is that all, sir? Can I go now?"

"Not quite," said the chief.

Finley glanced uneasily at the dragon to see if he were still slumped in his cell with his eyes closed. He was.

"Then after you've done that," continued the chief, "you will load the dragon into the truck and drive him to Yellowstone National Park."

Finley blinked and then shook his head slightly. "I'll do what, sir?" he asked.

"You'll load the dragon in the truck and drive him

73

to Yellowstone National Park" the chief repeated crossly.

"That's what I thought you said," said Finley, and he started to laugh a strange little laugh. "Drive him to Yellowstone National Park," he said over and over to himself. He saluted the door and started off in the opposite direction.

"No, no, *that* way," said the chief, turning Finley around and heading him in the right direction. He watched Finley wobble down the hall and then he sighed, "I don't know, mayor," he said. "It's not easy to get good men for the force these days. It'll be good to retire from all this."

But the mayor wasn't listening. "Well, that's that," he said, very pleased. "Now all we have to do is wait until it's dark. Then we can get this dragon out of here without anybody seeing. Once he's up in Yellowstone, we're rid of him for good. He's their problem then." And he laughed.

Then he and the chief slapped each other on the back, told each other how smart they both were, and left.

7

When the two men had gone, William hurried over to Darius' cell.

"Hey, Darius. Pst! Wake up!" he called. But Darius didn't move.

William tried calling to him again, but it was difficult. He couldn't call too loudly for he didn't want anyone to hear, and yet he had to warn his friend about the mayor's plan.

William picked up the yardstick Finley had dropped and put it through the bars of Darius' cell. He poked him several times with it. "Pst! Wake up! Hey, Darius!"

Darius stirred and let out a long, low growling moan.

William looked around to see if anyone had heard and was coming. "Sh!" he cautioned the dragon. But no one came, so William repeated his efforts to arouse the dragon.

Presently Darius' eyelids flickered and he opened his eyes.

"Hey, it's me!" said William. "Over here."

Darius frowned and tried to focus his eyes. Then he put his paw up to his forehead and moaned.

"Please hurry and wake up," William pleaded with the dragon.

"Here," he said, getting the box of corn flakes. "Eat these. They'll wake you up."

He pushed the box through the bars at Darius. When Darius didn't move, William shook the box and sprinkled corn flakes all over the dragon and the cell. Whenever the dragon moved, even slightly, it made a crunching noise. But still the dragon did not wake up completely.

William put some peanut butter on the banana. He stuck the banana on the end of the yardstick and poked it through the bars and waved it under Darius' nose. Darius sniffed.

"Pst! Darius!" William called. The dragon blinked his eyes and sniffed a few times, and then he slowly turned his head and looked directly at William. William smiled broadly. "Hey, man, you're awake," he said.

The dragon shook his head as if trying to clear it, took a few deep breaths, and then he looked around.

"Where am I?" he said, weakly.

"In jail," William said.

"In jail!" said the dragon, looking around at the steel bars and the tiny locked cell and trying to figure out what this meant. "You mean," he said, "that I've been put in the dungeon?"

William nodded.

The dragon stared at William a few minutes trying to clear his eyes and his mind. Presently he asked, "Sir William? Is that you?"

"It's me," grinned William.

"But what are *you* doing here?" asked Darius.

"I wanted to talk to you," he said.

"And what am *I* doing here?" the dragon thundered, trying to stand up. But the cell was too small for him and he bumped his head on the ceiling. "Ouch!" he cried.

"Sh!" said William. "You've got to be quiet, or else the guards will come."

"What guards?" said Darius. "What am I doing here?"

"Well, it's hard to explain," William began.

"And what are all of *these!*" Darius said, shaking himself.

"Corn flakes," said William.

Darius stared at William.

"Want some?" William asked, putting the box through the bars.

"No, I don't want some," Darius snapped. "I want out of here. That's what I want."

"I've got that figured out," said William helping himself to corn flakes. "I think I know how you can escape."

"Escape!" roared the dragon.

"Sh!" said William.

"Why should I escape," whispered Darius, "when I don't even know why I'm here?"

"This is upsetting me," Darius snarled. "I've never been put in a dungeon before in my life. Humiliating! I am a law-abiding dragon. How dare they put me in a dungeon!" And he tried to stand up again and bumped his head. "Ouch!" he growled. "Who's responsible for putting me here? And why am I here?" he demanded.

"Well—see—I guess you're not supposed to hit city property," William explained.

Darius thought a moment.

"The dozer bull?" he asked.

"Uh-huh," nodded William, "and you're not supposed to try to fight a policeman."

"The army of Kingdom of Establishment?" asked Darius, remembering.

William nodded. "It's a law. They have to—"

"But they were invading your Kingdom," said Darius.

"It's theirs, too," said William, offering Darius the banana with peanut butter on it.

Darius, who was trying hard to understand everything that William was saying, shook his head and waved away the banana impatiently.

"You mean," he said, frowning, "that the Kingdom of Park and the Kingdom of Establishment are not really two different kingdoms?"

"Well, they're different," said William.

"But not separate," said Darius, looking rather fiercely at William.

William shrugged and started to eat the banana with the peanut butter on it.

"And the policemen," he said, "are for both kingdoms?"

"Uh-huh," said William.

"Aha!" said Darius. "Hm, ah." And he sat thinking.

"But I've got a plan," said William, licking the peanut butter and banana off his fingers.

"How's that?" asked Darius, who was still thinking very hard.

"How you're going to escape," William said.

Darius stared at William a moment, still thinking. "I won't need to escape," he said, presently. "I will simply tell them that I thought the policemen were an invading army and then they'll let me out of here. Then I'll talk to King Mayor and I'll tell him to destroy the dozer bull. And that will be that."

"That won't work," said William.

"Why not?" asked Darius.

"Because the mayor and the police chief were talking. I heard them. And they said they were going to get rid of you."

"Get rid of *me?*" said the dragon, rising and bumping his head again. "Ouch! How?" he asked.

"They're going to drive you in a truck to Yellowstone where you won't be a problem," William said.

"Me, a problem?" Darius roared.

"Sh!" said William. But it was too late.

Two policemen came down the hall and William ran and hid behind the trash can.

"Pretend you're asleep!" he whispered to Darius.

"Why?" asked Darius.

"Because," William explained.

Darius shook his head. It was all to much for him to understand. He slumped down in his cell and shut his eyes.

The two policemen approached Darius' cell with caution.

"Looks quiet to me," whispered one.

"Yeah. Good thing, too," whispered the other.

"He's a big one, all right," said the first. "I wonder if he can blow fire?"

Darius gave a little snort and twitched his tail at this. The two men jumped back.

"Blow fire?" whispered the other, after a minute.

"Sure," the first answered. "I read somewhere once about dragons blowing fire."

The two men stared in silent wonder at Darius. He was growing very uncomfortable under their gaze when one said, "Well, I guess we'll never know. I hear they're getting rid of him tonight."

"Yeah," said the other. "Good thing, too. He gives me the creeps."

And the two policemen tiptoed back down the hall.

"Well," snorted Darius when he was sure they were gone. "So I give him the creeps, do I!" And he became very angry. "I'll give him more than that when I get out of here," he growled.

"Sh!" William said, coming out of his hiding place. "That's what we've got to talk about."

"What?" said Darius, still angry.

"How we're going to get you out of here," William said.

"Escape?" asked Darius.

"Uh-huh," William nodded.

"Never!" Darius thundered. "It's against my principles."

81

"Huh?" William was puzzled.

"I will talk to King Mayor and the one called Chief. And when they understand the truth of what has happened and the misunderstandings that caused it, they will pardon me and set me free from their dungeon," Darius said. And he took a large breath and nodded.

"But they don't want to talk to you," William said.

"Why not?" Darius asked.

"Because you're a dragon," said William. Darius squinted his eyes and looked a long time at William. "They said people would laugh if they saw them talking to a dragon," William added.

"Do you mean," he said after a few minutes, "that they don't like dragons?"

"I guess not," William shrugged.

Darius slumped down in his cell and brooded for some time.

"I don't really care if you can't blow fire," William said presently. "I mean—I guess you're a real dragon anyhow."

Darius looked over at William. "I am a real dragon," he said, softly, "and I am proud of it." Then he fell to thinking some more, so William let him alone.

William wandered around for a bit and looked down some halls and around some corners. There wasn't really very much to see and soon William went back to Darius' cell and sat down.

82

After awhile Darius said, "What is this plan of yours for my escape?"

"They'll bring a truck when it's dark," William began. And he leaned very close to Darius' cell and whispered into his ear. From time to time Darius would nod and say "hm" and "ah" and "so." At one point, he and William laughed very hard about something, and then William whispered some more.

Suddenly William turned around and listened. He heard sounds down the hall.

"Sh!" he said to Darius. "Somebody's coming." He swiftly disappeared behind the trash can. "Don't forget," he added, peering over the can at Darius.

"I won't," said Darius, and he slumped down and pretended to sleep.

Darius pretended to be asleep for awhile. But sitting with his eyes shut made it unnecessary to pretend. Soon he really was asleep and dreaming of his once peaceful, quiet life in his cave. It was a lovely dream, and he did not want to wake up when he heard something that sounded like keys being jangled in front of him.

He opened one eye and saw that it was now quite dark. He opened both eyes just enough to see several

men in the dim shadows, one of them working the lock on his cell.

"OK," said one man, his voice shaking. "I'll open the door, and you fellows take hold of him and we'll —that is, you will lead him out the back way."

Darius thought he recognized the voice. He squinted through half-opened eyes and in the dim light saw that it was indeed Finley. Darius smiled, recalling something William had told him earlier that had made them both laugh. He did not recognize the other two, but their shirts were lettered ALL AMERICAN MOVING COMPANY.

The big door to the cell opened with a dreadful grating screech.

"Quiet!" Finley yelled and jumped at the sound of his own voice. "Don't wake him up," he whispered to the others.

"How's it going?" asked the mayor, peering around the big doors.

"So far so good, sir," said Finley, not very convincingly.

"We'll be back here if you need help," said the chief, who was standing next to the mayor behind the big doors.

"That's good to know, sir," Finley said, and gave the chief a sickly grin.

When the cell door was all the way open, Finley nodded to the two moving men. They looked at each other and then shrugged and stepped into Darius' cell. This was very difficult for there wasn't very much room.

"Get him under the front legs," whispered Finley, flapping his own elbows to demonstrate.

"He ought to come peacefully," the chief said to the mayor. "Had no trouble getting him in here."

The mayor nodded. He felt reassured by the chief's words until the two moving men pulled Darius up and out of his cell. It was the first time the mayor had seen Darius in a standing position, and even with his neck and head slumped over in mock sleep, he was a formidable sight to behold.

"Great scott!" said the mayor, shrinking back. "Let's get him out of here right away!"

But just as the two movers began pushing and guiding Darius down a hall, William shouted, "Now," and sprang out from behind the trash can, tipping it over and sending it crashing down with a bang.

Finley fainted on the spot. Before anyone else could move, Darius had straightened up to his full height. The mayor gasped and flattened himself against the wall, trying to make himself as small as possible.

Darius lifted his front legs and raised the two movers off the ground. Then he sent both men sliding down the long hall like bowling balls. They slipped and slid all the way down the hall. Then before they'd even stopped sliding, they were running—around the corner, through the offices and outside, without once looking back.

Darius stood very still while William jumped on his back.

"Let's go!" William cried, and he steered Darius around a corner and down a corridor.

"Stop them!" called the chief, squinting to see where they had gone.

"Finley," he shouted, "blow your whistle!"

Finley raised up to a sitting position and blew a thin tweet on his whistle and then promptly fell back onto the floor.

"Which way did they go?" the chief bellowed.

"I don't know," gasped the mayor. "That way, I think," he said pointing in different directions with each arm.

"Never mind," snapped the chief. And he hurried to the main desk and called into a microphone. "Attention! Attention! This is the chief. All cars! All cars! A dragon and a little boy are loose somewhere in the city. Find them! What? Yes, I said a dragon. Throw everything you've got into this." Then, his voice changed, tears came to his eyes. "Please, boys," he pleaded, "don't let your chief down. Let him retire in peace—just a few more weeks to go." And he put the microphone down and sat limply in a chair. "Six more weeks," he muttered. "Six more weeks."

8

William perched on the dragon's neck just above his wings. "Hey, this is OK!" he cried excitedly. They raced through the halls, pounded down the stairs, skidded around corners, the dragon's claws squealing across the slick floors as they rounded the turns. William steered the dragon by patting Darius' neck first on one side, then on the other, depending on which way they were to turn as they sped past the city offices. "Duck!" he'd yell, when he saw a doorway coming.

They passed one guard at the exit, but he was so busy phoning his relatives in Dubuque to tell them about the dragon they had in City Hall that he didn't even see Darius and William whiz by.

Once they were out of the building and in the night

air, William breathed more easily. "We made it!" he shouted. "Let's go!"

So he steered Darius down some back alleys, through a cellar that ran under the fire department, and up on the top of a wall which went along the river, and then down along a railroad track. A couple of times they dashed in one door and out the other of an open freight car. As Darius jumped off a high place, he would spread his wings and glide a few feet. It was a thrilling ride for William.

They dashed up and down the hills of the city dump, hopping across old auto bodies, around the water tower, and across a bridge, until the poor dragon suddenly plopped down, exhausted.

William got off the dragon's neck and came around and looked into his face. "What's the matter?" he asked.

"Where are we going?" Darius panted.

He mopped his brow with his front leg. He looked at William who was not very big and he wondered why he was so heavy all of a sudden.

"You tired?" William asked.

"Very," said the dragon.

"OK, we can rest for awhile, I guess," said William. "It doesn't look as if they've followed us. But we'd better go down there," he said pointing to a big steel drainage pipe that came out under a road. He motioned for the dragon to follow him into the ditch and into the pipe.

Darius did not like the looks of this place very much, but he hadn't liked much of anything that he'd seen around this strange kingdom since he came out of his cave. So he simply sat down in the mud and water at the bottom of the pipe and panted, for he was very tired.

William sat down next to him. Off in the distance they could hear the sirens wailing up one street and down another.

After awhile William held out the box of corn flakes to Darius.

"Want some?" he said.

"Do you eat all the time?" Darius asked William, who was taking a handful for himself.

William shrugged and crunched away.

Darius sighed and took some out for himself. He found he was actually very hungry. He looked at the strange tan flakes and thought how he would enjoy sinking his teeth into a nice juicy elm root down in his cave about now.

But he sighed and ate the corn flakes. Then he and William sat in silence for some time listening to the sirens coming and going.

After awhile William said, "I think we'd better go."

Darius had dozed off for a moment, and now he felt a little better.

"Where are we going?" he asked as William climbed back on his neck.

91

"I don't know," said William. "I'm trying to think."

"See here," said the dragon, "I can't keep escaping forever. It's not proper for one thing," he said, "and besides, it's very tiring."

"Well, we could go back to the park," William said. "I know lots of good hiding places around there."

"The park? Yes! Yes!" cried the dragon. He was very pleased. "I want to go back where my cave is."

"Hey, hold it! Hold it!" cried William, for Darius bounded out of the drainage tunnel and down the street nearly throwing him off.

"Is this the right way?" he called back to William as he raced across a lot and through a half-built factory.

"I—I guess so," William said. He wasn't sure where they were now. But all at once he saw a building he thought he recognized. "Turn here," he yelled to Darius.

"Right-o," said Darius, rounding the corner.

"No, no, the other way!" cried William tugging at the dragon's neck trying to steer him.

But it was too late. Darius had been so anxious to see his cave again that he hadn't paid much attention to William's directions, and he turned into a football stadium. Unfortunately, a game was being played. The referee had just called a time out when Darius and William charged across the field. Everyone in the grandstands stood and cheered when they saw William and Darius race down the field right between the goal posts.

Everyone sat down and said that the half-time activities were getting better and better every year.

It is not easy for a dragon to run about a city unnoticed and find hiding places at just the right time and just the right size.

At the approach of a car, any car, Darius did all manner of desperate things. Once, just in the nick of time, he threw himself on the ground behind a tall hedge by a library, curling his tail over his back so it wouldn't stick out. He got a crick in his tail from that, and William had to rub it out quickly before they could go on.

Another time he ducked into an empty warehouse as a police car rounded the corner ahead. The car parked right in front and they had to run upstairs to the roof. The car didn't move so Darius spread his leathery wings and jumped. He glided for several blocks to a very hard landing and decided not to do that again.

But on and on William and Darius hurried, ducking into the deserted lobby of a big apartment building, hiding in the frozen food warehouse of a supermarket—that was cold! They slipped into an empty school bus parked in front of a high school and stretched out on the floor while three police cars rushed by. They trotted alongside a big cross-country truck-and-trailer rig with a police car

93

cruising along on the other side, until the police car turned off on a side street.

When the tired old dragon finally spotted the familiar park, he leaped for joy.

"Hey, watch it!" William cried, finding it very hard to ride a dragon after all.

"Sorry," said the dragon, and stopped leaping.

However, he did gallop across the park to the hole at the entrance of his cave without so much as looking to see if he were now followed. Even though it was filled with rocks and dirt and debris, the dragon shed a tear when he saw his old familiar home.

"I'm home," he said, gratefully. He moved a few rocks and sat down happily in the hole.

William climbed down from Darius's neck and ran around to face the dragon. "You can't sit here!" he said.

"Why not?" asked Darius. "I live here."

"But they'll find you," William cried.

"So?" said the dragon.

William blinked and stared at Darius. "You've got to hide," he said.

Darius shook his head. "I won't hide, and I won't run away ever again, and I have finished escaping," he said. "All I wanted to do was to get back to my home," he added. "And now that I'm here, I don't intend to leave." Darius put his arms behind his long neck and leaned back against the sides of the hole and looked up at the stars.

"You know, Sir William," he said thoughtfully, "once, on this very spot, you could see those same stars much clearer than you can see them now. A pity, a pity."

William looked up at the sky. "I can see them," he said, looking at the stars.

"Too many buildings," said Darius, "and the air— what have you done to the air?"

William was looking up at the stars when he heard the siren. He looked at Darius and saw that his friend really meant what he said. He did not intend to move. The siren faded, and William sighed in relief. But then he saw a police car that had no siren and no flashing red or yellow lights drive up to the curb and stop.

"They're here," he cried to Darius, tugging at his arm.

"I expected them," said Darius, calmly, not taking his eyes off the stars.

William turned to look and sure enough, he saw the police chief and the mayor get out, followed at some distance by Finley, who had been driving.

"Aw phooey!" William said, unhappily. And he sat in the dirt next to his friend and waited.

9

The mayor glanced around the park nervously. "You're sure your idea about talking to this dragon will work?" he asked the chief.

"Well, it seems the fairest thing to do—and the quietest," said the chief.

"Yes, we must be careful to keep this as quiet as we can," the mayor said. "We don't want any bad publicity."

"Nothing to worry about," said the chief. Then he chortled. "I had a feeling he'd show up here."

"It seems to me," said the mayor, as if trying to re-assure himself, "that dragons would be reasonable creatures, if you were reasonable with them."

"Well, that's the way I have it figured," said the chief, sounding a little nervous himself. "I mean, he brushed

Finley off when he threw him in the dirt. You don't see that very often."

"True," said the mayor. "And Yellowstone is a very nice place."

"Yup. Emma and I—that's the wife—we always like it," the chief said.

"We'd better be able to talk to him," said the mayor, "because if there's any trouble, there goes your retirement and my re-election."

The chief nodded slowly. "Six weeks—only six weeks to go and that stupid bulldozer had to unearth a dragon."

The farther they walked into the park, the slower they moved.

"You're sure your men know what to do in case—in case he causes trouble?" the mayor asked.

"Oh, sure," the chief said uneasily, knowing his men did not wish to tangle with a dragon. "I'll give a signal, the men will come and Finley will go get the truck, and it will all work out," he said, his voice dwindling a bit at the end.

The chief squinted across the dark park. "Should be near the bulldozer," he said. "Carson said he saw them going that way."

"The bulldozer's over there," the mayor said, pointing in another direction.

"Oh," said the chief, and changed his course.

As they approached the silent bulldozer, the mayor

looked around uneasily. "You're sure your men know the signal?" he whispered hoarsely to the chief.

Now the mayor could see the dragon leaning against the side of the hole and looking up at the stars. William was sitting next to him with his head down, glumly drawing in the dirt with a stick.

"There they are! There they are!" whispered the mayor, grabbing the chief.

"Where?" whispered the chief, squinting into the darkness.

"In that hole," rasped the Mayor, pointing to the excavation.

"Good evening, gentlemen," Darius said.

The mayor and the chief exchanged startled looks and stared down at the dragon.

"I've been expecting you," Darius added.

At that moment Louie and the group of young people came running up. "What's going on?" they asked. They lived nearby and had seen the chief and the mayor drive up. "Hey, it's Darius!" Louie shouted happily, and the young people cheered.

"Ah, King Jazz," Darius greeted Louie, "I was hoping you'd come."

"Now see here," the mayor said. He had not planned on this. He had practiced what he was going to do and say to the dragon, for he always practiced his speeches in case the newspapers or the television cameras were around, and he did not want anyone changing his plans.

"We're here on official business," he snapped. "You youngsters run along."

"Let them stay," said the dragon as he stood up. "I have something to say to all of you!"

"You have something to say!" huffed the mayor. But then he saw the dragon rising to his full height and muttered, "Yes, yes, of course."

Darius stood on the ground next to the hole and looked down into it.

"That was my home," the dragon said sadly, pointing at the hole, and turning next to stare directly at the mayor.

The mayor swallowed hard and cleared his throat nervously and said yes, he had heard about that.

"Then you know why your dozer bull must be destroyed," said Darius.

The mayor was very upset. This whole thing was not going at all the way he had planned it. At this rate he'd never get to give his speech.

"You don't understand," he said. And he turned to the chief. "Tell him about Yellowstone."

"Me?" said the chief.

"Yes," said the mayor, rattled. "I've forgotten what I was going to say."

"Well," said the chief, clearing his throat and rising to the occasion. "You see, uh, dragon, it's this way. The mayor here feels that having a dragon around town wouldn't be good for the image. Not at all good."

"That's right," the mayor added quickly.

"And I go along with that. I mean, a city's got enough problems without having a dragon," the chief said. "Now, I don't want to hurt your feelings . . ."

"No, no," the mayor assured the dragon.

"But, well, we've come up with a little plan."

"That's right," said the mayor.

Darius stood watching them silently.

"Uh, you tell him," the chief said to the mayor.

"Me?" asked the mayor. The chief nodded.

"Well, all right," the mayor sighed. He took a deep breath and remembering some of his speech, he began. He talked for some time about the pleasures awaiting the dragon in Yellowstone, and then he stopped to see the reaction it was having. But there was none. Only the chief nodded pleasantly to him.

"I heard that you wanted to get rid of me," Darius said. Before the mayor could say anything, Darius went on. "But this is my home. I will not leave it. You needn't worry that I'll cause trouble in your city. It is a noisy, smelly, ugly, disagreeable place and I would not live in it."

The mayor looked relieved and he and the chief nodded to each other.

"It was such a beautiful place here, once," Darius said, looking out across the horizon. "Rolling green meadows dotted with wild flowers, fresh bright air and clear streams, and deep forests with tall, silent trees." He sighed, then looked back at the mayor and then at Louie. "I have been doing some thinking," he said, "and it seems to me that your two kingdoms should get together to save what is left before it is all destroyed, forever."

Louie and the mayor looked at each other.

"Well, I think that's a good idea," said the mayor, "but it's just not that easy."

"What isn't?" said the dragon.

"Getting together," said Louie.

"Why is that?" Darius asked.

"Well," Louie said, "see—we got this generation gap thing going."

"What's that?" asked Darius.

"It's like—we don't dig each other," Louie said.

"We don't understand each other," explained the mayor.

"Why not?" Darius asked.

"Well, they're older and they don't understand us," Louie said.

"And they're younger and don't understand *us,*" added the mayor.

The dragon looked at the two, and then he put his long neck back and laughed and laughed until he had to wipe his eyes.

"But there are only twenty or thirty years' difference between you," he said. "What is that? I am a thousand years older than both of you! Do you think such a little time as twenty years is important?" He laughed again. "It is only *that,*" he said, giving a little snap with his fingers. "From what I have seen around here, before you know what has happened," he said to Louie, "you will be his age and wanting to build parking lots, and he will be an old man wanting a park to sun himself in." Then he laughed again. "What foolishness!"

"Enough of this nonsense," he said after he wiped his eyes again and took a handkerchief and blew his nose. "Now," he said fastening a hard gaze on the mayor. "What does your Kingdom of Establishment do with all its power? Do you do what's best for everybody, and for those in the future? Do you think about the need to see beauty and green living things, and to breathe good air and drink clean water, and to have quiet, restful places where one can think undisturbed thoughts? Do you use your power for your people this way?" he thundered. "Or do you plow under your last remaining green parks and make parking lots for those hordes of honking monsters on your roads?"

The mayor cleared his throat and shifted uncomfortably from one foot to the other.

"You have very strange customs," the dragon said. "You fence in your parks and let your cities grow. It would seem more sensible if it were the other way around."

"Hooray!" cheered the young people.

"And *you,*" Darius said, now turning to stare coldly at Louie and the young people. "When you do have a park in which to play, what do you do to keep it nice? What are those papers and bits of half-eaten lunches that I see dumped on the ground and blowing around? Shameful! Disgraceful! Tell me, do you use those strong muscles of yours to plant new grass where your shoes have scuffed it away? Do you plant a flower where your games have trampled others? Or," he thundered, "do you ruin what you have and howl for more?"

Louie shrugged and kicked at a rock with his toe.

Darius went up a dirt mound to where the bulldozer was. He took out his sword and said, "And now will you destroy your dozer bull, or shall I?"

The mayor blinked and stared openmouthed at Darius. Then he grinned and turned to the chief and winked. "I don't think that will do it," he said, nodding at Darius' sword.

"This dozer bull is destroying my home," said Darius. "When it's rested up tomorrow morning, it will start again. I say, will you destroy it or must I?"

"Well, neither one of us will," said the mayor, humoring the dragon. "You see, the dozer bull—I mean, the bulldozer is a very helpful machine. It helps build all kinds of things."

"I have no doubt the beast could be trained to build as well as destroy," Darius said. "Surely it is the fault of its masters that it does what it does."

"Well, yes. That's probably so," said the mayor, uncomfortably. "But sometimes it has to destroy something before it can build something else."

"I see," said the dragon. "It must destroy my home and this park before it can build a parking lot. Is that what you mean?"

"Well, something like that," the mayor muttered.

"So you do not intend to destroy your dozer bull?" asked Darius.

"That's right," said the mayor. "We will not destroy the dozer bull—uh, the bulldozer."

"Then I shall have to do it as a warning to all of you to choose carefully what you destroy and what you build." Darius raised his sword. "Stand back," he said.

"This ought to be good," the mayor whispered to the chief as he nudged him in the ribs. "We'll let him take a crack at this and then we'll start him off to Yellowstone."

The chief nodded and said, "Good enough."

But just as Darius was about to bring his raised sword down with a vengeance on the bulldozer, William rushed up to him and threw his arms around him. "It won't work," he cried, "You'll just get hurt. And then they'll laugh at you." Two large tears slowly rolled down William's cheeks, and he could not stop them, try as he might.

The dragon looked down at his small friend for a moment. And suddenly he had an idea. "I won't be hurt," he said, gently. "And I don't think they'll laugh either!"

He nodded to William to stand back, and William did as he was told. Darius put down his sword and walked up to the bulldozer. He stood in front of it and breathed in and out loudly, and huffed and snorted and puffed and blew for several minutes.

"What's he doing?" asked the mayor

"Beats me," said the chief.

But William knew. He jumped up and down and clapped his hands. "Come on, Darius!" he shouted. "I know you can do it!"

"Do what?" asked the mayor.

All at once a gigantic flash of bright orange-red lighted up the sky and made the entire park seem as if it were daylight.

"What is it?" gasped the mayor, falling to the ground and covering his eyes.

"I don't know," yelled the chief, racing behind a tree.

Finley, who had been standing back at the curbing next to the police car, hid in the back seat.

"Hooray!" cried the young people. "It's the Fourth of July!"

"No! it's the *dragon!*" cried the mayor, peeking out between his fingers.

It was indeed the dragon. Darius was blowing great spurts of fire from his nostrils.

Suddenly Darius gave a final fiery blow, followed by a large grey clouds of smoke, and then the exhausted dragon fell back onto the dirt.

There was a moment of stunned silence.

"He melted it!" one boy exclaimed.

"He melted it?" asked the mayor, raising his head. "He melted it? He melted the bulldozer!" he cried out.

Sure enough, where once a mighty bulldozer had stood, there was now only a small heap of melted steel, smoking and cooling in the night air.

"I knew you could do it. I knew you could," shouted William, running up to Darius. "I knew you were a real dragon!"

"Didn't I always say I was?" said Darius, weakly.

"Wa—wa—well, well," stuttered the mayor, picking himself up. He carefully inspected the smoking pile of junk, first from one side, then from the other. "Uh, hmmm. Well, well, well. Heh, heh." He looked long and hard at the heap that was once a powerful machine. Then he looked at Darius. "Well, I believe we have somewhat changed our plans, haven't we, chief?"

The chief nodded frantically.

"Instead of a parking lot," said the mayor. "I think we should keep this a park. Don't you, chief?"

"Oh, absolutely!" said the chief, coming from around the tree. "No question in my mind about it."

"And we ought to clean it up, right now!" said Louie quickly. All the young people scurried around in the dark, picking up papers and all the time keeping a wary eye out for Darius, fearful he might melt something else.

"And there's no reason," the mayor hastened to add, "not to start repairing our friend's—that is, the dragon's home—right away. Is there?" Everyone agreed.

While the dragon rested, Louie and William and all the young people, the mayor and the chief and Finley, whom the chief sent one of the boys to get, and several other policemen who came running when they saw the flash of light worked together on the dragon's tunnel. They carried away the rocks, moved boulders, shoveled the loose dirt, carried away the debris, and made repairs on the sides of the tunnel.

With all of them working together, it was no time at all before Darius' tunnel was back in shape—the way it was before the bulldozer smashed into it early that morning. What's more, there wasn't a loose paper or bit of trash anywhere to be found, either in the park or on any of the streets around it.

10

When all was neat and orderly, everyone lined up alongside the tunnel entrance, smiling nervously, hoping the dragon would approve. Darius looked around at the group of tired, dirty boys and men, and then stretched and yawned and got to his feet. He walked over to his tunnel and inspected it carefully, and then he looked around the park.

"I hope," he growled, "that this cleaning job was not done simply to send me back into my cave." The mayor and the others quickly assured him that it was not.

But the dragon looked around the group and was not convinced. "Hm," he said, "well, just in case it was, I think I will come out of my cave and pay a visit to you, here in this park, every year on my birthday. Yes, that's a good idea. One doesn't like to spend one's birthday alone. And I would like to visit with my friend," he said, patting William on the head, "and all of you."

"Well, that sounds like a very good idea," said the mayor, and he and the chief nodded to each other. "When is your birthday?"

"I can't remember, it's been so long ago. But I'll just come whenever I feel I want a birthday party," the dragon said.

All the young people cheered at this, for they were fond of birthday parties.

The mayor swallowed hard and cleared his throat and said that would probably be very nice. Then he thought about it some more and began thinking of all the speeches he could give and all the parades he could ride in on such occasions. "Yes, yes," he said, happily, "and we'll call it Darius Day and have a big celebration right here in the park!"

"You can have a giant cake with a thousand candles on it!" cried William.

"What a blast!" Louie shouted.

"And you can blow them all out!" yelled one of the boys.

"Yes," said the dragon, "I will like that." For, being a peaceful dragon, he much preferred to blow out flames than to make them.

"And I will play my tuba!" said the chief, thinking

110

ahead to when he would be retired and have enough time to take up his music lessons again.

Thus it is, once every year, in a certain park in a certain city, Darius the dragon comes out of his cave to celebrate his birthday. You will know what park this is if you are ever there, because of the birthday present the people of the city gave to Darius. There in the park, on the very spot where once the bulldozer stood, is a giant statue of Darius and the dozer bull.

ABOUT THE AUTHOR

A native of Iowa, Eleanor Brown was a professional actress, majoring in theater arts at the University of California at Los Angeles when she met Ray Harder, an English major with a bent for poetry. Of the years at UCLA she has written, "I helped form and acted in a theatrical company that toured Southern California. This same company began to include children's plays in its repertory, and it was then that I started working with the man who later became my husband."

The team of Ray and Eleanor Harder is best known for joint efforts in writing and adapting musical plays. For Ray, an advertising executive, writing is a hobby. For Mrs. Harder writing is a profession, and she has produced scripts, stories, and music for both commercial and educational television and radio. *Darius and the Dozer Bull* is her first book.

The Harders have a son and a daughter. As a family they enjoy theater and music and, again as a family, they have produced and toured with two of their own plays. Other interests include sailing and animals, especially Henry, a hundred-pound red collie, and Belle Williams, a smart cat that wandered in and stayed.

ABOUT THE ARTIST

Davis K. Stone's drawings have appeared in more than a hundred books and in many national magazines. Before he received recognition as an illustrator he had earned a degree at the University of Oregon and had done further work and study at *Universidad de Michoacan,* Mexico, and at the Art Center at Los Angeles.

Born in Oregon, Mr. Stone now lives in Port Washington, New York. He has served as vice-president of the Society of Illustrators and is the author-illustrator of the book *Art in Advertising.*